Zack, Jess, and their grandparents and parents were going to the Steam Fair. It was held in the village next to where Zack and Jess's grandparents lived. Their grandparents, Gran and Gramps, helped out at the fair and Zack and Jess loved going there.

I0824947

The fair was on for an entire weekend and Zack and Jess loved looking at all of the old steam engines. "Just imagine seeing one of those on a farm or mending a road," said Zack.

Smoke drifted across the fairground, as Zack and Jess ran to where the engines were. Dad and Gramps strolled along behind them.

Zack and Jess stood and looked up at the first steam engine in the line. Smoke was just beginning to puff out from the funnel. A man with his face, cap and overalls all covered in black smudges from the coal, soot, and smoke waved and called to their grandfather.

“Morning, Sid! Nice to see you again. And you two!” he smiled and nodded at Zack and Jess. “We’ve just lit the boiler and we’re getting the steam up ready for our first ride around the ring. Perhaps you two would like to join me later for the Tortoise Race?”

“Yes please!” shouted Zack and Jess together. “See you later!”

They continued on, looking at all the engines. They stopped at the steam thresher. As wheat was being forked in at one end, the grain was separated and dropped into a sack. Then the straw came out and piled up at the other end.

“All of this, plus the cutting, is carried out by just one combine harvester now,” remarked Dad.

Further along, Zack and Jess stopped to look at an old fire engine. A firefighter explained that it would have had horses harnessed to it, and the horses would have raced the engine to a fire. Instead of a siren, a big bell would have been rung to let everyone know the engine was coming and to get out of the way.

Zack and Jess climbed up onto the engine. Zack sat in the driver's seat and pretended to drive.

Once they had climbed down, Jess announced that she was going to the main ring, as there was a display by a dog agility team. She and Zack found a space and sat on some straw bales, waiting for the display to start. The dogs were very excited and were barking and jumping. They couldn't wait to get started.

There was a set of obstacles around the ring. The dogs had to run and jump over some hurdles, go into a tunnel and out the other end, run up a plank, balance at the top, and then run down the other side.

Next they had to climb up some stairs, stop, and sit until their owner told them to carry on. Then they had to weave in and out of a set of poles and race to the finish line. Everyone clapped and cheered as the dogs finished.

Zack, Jess, Dad, and Gramps looked around some of the stalls. They were selling all sorts of things: bits of engines, tools, kites, clothes, and things for the garden.

Jess got a kite. Zack got some homemade fudge and Gramps got a strange bit of metal he said would fit a broken engine he had in his shed at home.

“Don’t let Gran see you with that!” said Jess.

The family made their way back to the big tea tent, where Gran and their mother were serving teas, coffees, cakes, and sandwiches.
"Hello," they said. "Looks like there has been quite a crowd in here," remarked their father.

"Yes," said Gran, "and I need some volunteers to collect cups and any rubbish left on the tables."
Zack and Jess set off to help, and soon all of the tables were cleared.

"Thank you," said Gran. "I think you deserve a turn on the funfair rides, don't you?"
"Yes!" yelled Zack and Jess, jumping about in excitement. Off they rushed to the corner of the park where the funfair was.

First, they went to the big slide. They climbed up the stairs to the top of the tall tower.
"Look! You can see everything from here," said Jess.
Then they sat on their mats and whooshed down and around until they flew off the bottom of the slide, giggling.

They tried the coconut stall next. Zack hit one of the coconuts and it wobbled but didn't fall. Jess took her three balls and threw them at the same coconut. Her third ball smacked into it, knocking it off its stand and onto the ground.

"Hooray!" they both shouted.

Jess got to keep the coconut she had knocked down.

"Time for more fun," said Jess, and they headed to the steam merry-go-round. It had brightly patterned horses on golden poles galloping around it.
"My favorite!" said their mother as she came up behind them.

They each climbed onto a horse and waited for the ride to start. A merry tune played, and the horses started to go up and down as they went around and around and got quicker and quicker.

After that, they got an ice cream, which they ate while listening to the Signing Singers. This band signed every song they sang.

Jess's friend, Beth, was one of the singers. She had joined because her brother, Sam, was deaf. The whole family had learned to sign so that they could talk to Sam.

"They are really good. I enjoyed that," said Jess.

"We need to be back at the main ring at four o'clock," said Gramps. They arrived just as the heavy horses and carts were leaving. Once they were out of the ring, all of the steam engines started to roll in. They puffed their way around the edge of the ring until they were in a line across the bottom.

"Let's hear you!" shouted the announcer over the loudspeaker. All of the engines tooted their whistles. They were very loud!

“Time for the race you have all been waiting for!” continued the announcer. “The Tortoise Race. The engines have to go as slowly as they can, without stopping, and the last one to cross the line is the winner,” he explained.

Gramps’ friend, Jim, waved at Zack and Jess. Gramps took them across and helped them scramble up into the cab of the steam engine.

Off they went. Zack and Jess took the wheel and steered together. They were going very, very slowly. Some of the other engines couldn't go as slowly and were soon ahead. The one next to them was doing really well, but made a mistake and stopped, so it was out.

The engine Zack and Jess were on ended up coming first.
"That was fun," said Zack. "Thank you for letting us take part in the race, Jim!"
"We'll have to come back next time and see if we can win again!" chuckled Jess.